The European Union

Political, Social, and Economic Cooperation

EUROPEAN UNION

POLITICAL, SOCIAL, AND ECONOMIC COOPERATION

The European Union

Political, Social, and Economic Cooperation

HUNGARY

by
Heather Docalavich

Mason Crest Publishers
Philadelphia

Mason Crest Publishers Inc.
370 Reed Road, Broomall, Pennsylvania 19008
(866) MCP-BOOK (toll free)
www.masoncrest.com

First printing
1 2 3 4 5 6 7 8 9 10

Library of Congress Cataloging-in-Publication Data

Docalavich, Heather.
  Hungary / by Heather Docalavich.
      p. cm.—(The European Union: political, social, and economic cooperation)
  Includes bibliographical references and index.
    ISBN 1-4222-0050-7
    ISBN 1-4222-0038-8 (series)
  1. Hungary—Juvenile literature. 2. European Union—Hungary—Juvenile literature. I. Title. II. European Union (Series) (Philadelphia, Pa.)
    DB906.D63 2006
    943.9—dc22
                                    2005014303

Produced by Harding House Publishing Service, Inc.
www.hardinghousepages.com
Interior design by Benjamin Stewart.
Cover design by MK Bassett-Harvey.
Printed in the Hashemite Kingdom of Jordan.

CONTENTS

HUNGARY

European Union Member since 2004

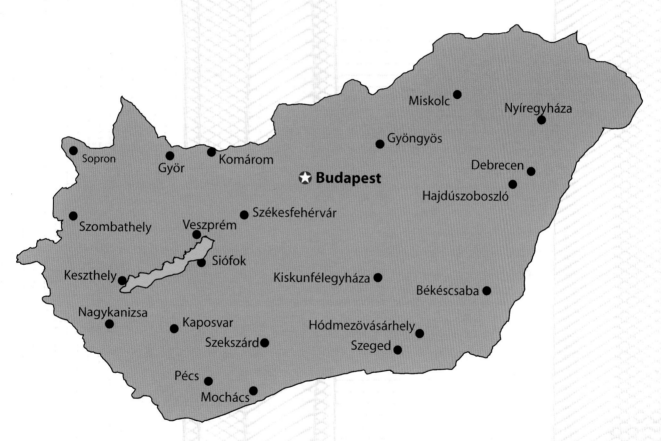

INTRODUCTION

Sixty years ago, Europe lay scarred from the battles of the Second World War. During the next several years, a plan began to take shape that would unite the countries of the European continent so that future wars would be inconceivable. On May 9, 1950, French Foreign Minister Robert Schuman issued a declaration calling on France, Germany, and other European countries to pool together their coal and steel production as "the first concrete foundation of a European federation." "Europe Day" is celebrated each year on May 9 to commemorate the beginning of the European Union (EU).

The EU consists of twenty-five countries, spanning the continent from Ireland in the west to the border of Russia in the east. Eight of the ten most recently admitted EU member states are former communist regimes that were behind the Iron Curtain for most of the latter half of the twentieth century.

Any European country with a democratic government, a functioning market economy, respect for fundamental rights, and a government capable of implementing EU laws and policies may apply for membership. Bulgaria and Romania are set to join the EU in 2007. Croatia and Turkey have also embarked on the road to EU membership.

While the EU began as an idea to ensure peace in Europe through interconnected economies, it has evolved into so much more today:

- Citizens can travel freely throughout most of the EU without carrying a passport and without stopping for border checks.

- EU citizens can live, work, study, and retire in another EU country if they wish.

- The euro, the single currency accepted throughout twelve of the EU countries (with more to come), is one of the EU's most tangible achievements, facilitating commerce and making possible a single financial market that benefits both individuals and businesses.

- The EU ensures cooperation in the fight against cross-border crime and terrorism.

- The EU is spearheading world efforts to preserve the environment.

- As the world's largest trading bloc, the EU uses its influence to promote fair rules for world trade, ensuring that globalization also benefits the poorest countries.

- The EU is already the world's largest donor of humanitarian aid and development assistance, providing 55 percent of global official development assistance to developing countries in 2004.

The EU is neither a nation intended to replace existing nations, nor an international organization. The EU is unique—its member countries have established common institutions to which they delegate some of their sovereignty so that decisions on matters of joint interest can be made democratically at the European level.

Europe is a continent with many different traditions and languages, but with shared values such as democracy, freedom, and social justice, cherished values well known to North Americans. Indeed, the EU motto is "United in Diversity."

Enjoy your reading. Take advantage of this chance to learn more about Europe and the EU!

Ambassador John Bruton,
Head of Delegation of the European Commission, Washington, D.C.

Lake Balaton is Central Europe's largest lake, famous as a resort and for the curative power of its nearby mineral springs.

1 CHAPTER THE LANDSCAPE

Welcome to Hungary, an ancient European nation. Covering an area of 35,919 square miles (93,030 sq. kilometers), Hungary is bordered on the north by Slovakia; on the northeast by Ukraine; on the east by Romania; on the south by Slovenia, Croatia, Serbia, and Montenegro; and on the west by Austria.

The Danube River stretches from the north, where it delineates the Hungarian-Slovakian border, to the border with Yugoslavia in the south. The bridge pictured above is in Esztergom, one of the former capitals of Hungary.

Hungary is landlocked, surrounded by mountain ranges on all sides, including the Alps, the Carpathians, and the Dinara Mountains. These mountains surround a vast, sweeping plain. Two-thirds of Hungary is comprised of this flat, low-lying land that is just slightly above sea level. Two large rivers, the Danube, and the Tisza, cross Hungary from north to south.

PLAINS, MOUNTAINS, AND FORESTS

Hungary is not a large country, but it does have a diverse landscape. The terrain has been shaped by a variety of both human and natural forces, and the results are some of the most unique natural areas in Europe. The European Union (EU) has classified Hungary as an independent biogeographical region. This is an important classification, as it will affect the kinds of funds available to Hungary for environmental protection.

The Great Hungarian Plain, or *Nagyalfold*, comprises most of the territory east of the Danube, and covers more than 50 percent of the entire country. The area in the center of the Great Plain is known as the *Puszta*, and is an extremely flat region of grassland. The surrounding regions of the plain are used for growing wheat and fruit. The entire area is used for grazing.

Transdanubia is the area to the west of the Danube near the Austrian border. Here, the terrain is varied, with mountainous areas in the south, some forested regions, and in the northwest, another small area of flat land known as the Little Plain or *Kisalfold*. Lake Balaton, a popular resort area, is the largest lake in Central Europe, and lies in the center of Transdanubia.

Most of Hungary's border regions are mountainous, and in the Matra Range of northern Hungary, the mountains were shaped by volcanic activity. The country is also known for its hot springs, with nearly eighty different springs identified in the capital city of Budapest alone. Hungary is also home to the largest **thermal lake** in the world, Lake Heviz.

RIVERS AND LAKES

Waterways have traditionally been a lifeline in Hungary, with the major river systems being an important source of transport throughout Hungarian history. Hungary's many lakes and rivers also provide important irrigation to the Great Plain, which has historically been susceptible to periods of drought.

The most important river is the Danube. Both a busy transport waterway and an important draw for tourists and water sport enthusiasts, it flows from its source in the Black Forest region of Germany, through Austria and Hungary, before reaching the Black Sea in Romania. A series of canals connect the Danube to other important rivers for transport. These include the Main, the Oder, and the Rhine rivers. The Danube also provides a transport line between the North Sea and the Black Sea, so its importance to Hungarian trade is vital. It also provides many miles of marshland, home to a variety of plant and animal life. The Tisza is another river crucial to Hungarian transportation and agriculture.

Hungary is also dotted with several lakes. The largest lake is Lake Balaton, and many other important lakes can be found across Hungary. These lakes that are scattered across the plain are the remains of a prehistoric sea that once covered the region. The many lakes and rivers give Hungarians and foreign visitors opportunities to enjoy swimming, boating, and other water sports.

A TEMPERATE CLIMATE

Hungary has a continental climate with cold, windy winters and warm to hot summer temperatures. Temperatures vary from highs near 95°F (35°C) in summer to lows of −20°F (−29°C) in winter. The average yearly rainfall is about twenty-four inches (600 millimeters).

Winter and summer are short, with longer spring and autumn seasons. The long, warm autumn extends the growing season and helps to produce excellent fruit crops and sweet wine grapes. This weather phenomenon is known as *Venasszonyok Nyara,* or "Old Ladies' Summer."

TREES, PLANTS, AND WILDLIFE

Most of the forests are found in the mountain areas or in the lower altitudes of Transdanubia. **Deciduous** trees such as beech, oak, and acacia are the main types of trees found in the lower woodlands, with **conifers** growing on higher altitudes. The Puszta is home to a great variety of wildflowers and grasses, while the rivers and their marshlands

The waters of Lake Balaton are comparatively warm, and are threatened by invasive plant species not native to the lake.

Fishing is a popular pastime in Hungary, especially around Lake Balaton.

produce many varieties of woody plants and reeds. The Danube is known for its water lilies in particular.

Hungary's wildlife includes deer, foxes, hare, and squirrels. Wild boars, wolves, jackals, lynx, and beavers are also found. The meadow viper is a poisonous snake found here. Tourists enjoy the many different species of **migratory** birds that cross the country; some of the most famous of these are the black stork and the eastern white pelican. The many lakes and rivers are home to a number of different fish, and fishing is a popular pastime.

Environmental protection has a long history in Hungary. The first environmental legislation, the Nature Protection Act, was passed in 1910. Today, many of the environmental laws are stricter in Hungary than measures provided under EU legislation. Approximately 10 percent of Hungary's territory is formally set aside for protection in ten national parks and several different Protected Landscape areas.

Hungary has a long and proud history as an independent nation. This monument, erected in 1896 at the entrance of Budapest's City Park, marks the millennium of the Magyar conquest of the region.

2 CHAPTER

HUNGARY'S HISTORY AND GOVERNMENT

Hungary's history is one of conquering armies and struggles for power and control. The land of Hungary has gone back and forth between cultures and ruling powers for centuries. Today, the Magyar people of Hungary are proud of their diverse heritage and have emerged from thousands of years of turmoil as a stable and peaceful democracy, ready to take their rightful place as an integral part of the European community.

ANCIENT HUNGARY

The lands of the Carpathian Basin, now known as Hungary, had been settled for thousands of years before the arrival of the Magyar tribes from which modern Hungarians are descended. A thriving **Bronze Age** culture existed in the region until invading horsemen from Asia wiped them out in the thirteenth century BCE. **Celts** later moved in and occupied the land, only to be conquered by the Romans, who divided the territory into the imperial provinces of Pannonia and Dacia.

In the fourth century, the **Goths** drove the Romans out of the area—but the Huns in turn conquered the Goths, when the famous Attila the Hun made the region famous as the center of his empire. After Attila's death, the area was settled by a variety of different tribes, including the Avars, Bulgars, Germans, and Slavs. The invading Magyars quickly conquered these tribes. As cavalrymen using Asian-style bows and arrows, the Magyars easily prevailed in battle and enslaved or **assimilated** the remaining population.

DATING SYSTEMS AND THEIR MEANING

You might be accustomed to seeing dates expressed with the abbreviations BC or AD, as in the year 1000 BC or the year AD 1900. For centuries, this dating system has been the most common in the Western world. However, since BC and AD are based on Christianity (BC stands for Before Christ and AD stands for *anno Domini*, Latin for "in the year of our Lord"), many people now prefer to use abbreviations that people from all religions can be comfortable using. The abbreviations BCE (meaning Before Common Era) and CE (meaning Common Era) mark time in the same way (for example, 1000 BC is the same year as 1000 BCE, and AD 1900 is the same year as 1900 CE), but BCE and CE do not have the same religious overtones as BC and AD.

THE MAGYARS

Modern historians dispute the origins of the Magyar people, but they likely came from somewhere between the Ural Mountains and the Volga River in what is now modern Russia. In ancient times, the Magyars likely existed as **nomadic** hunters and gatherers. Over the centuries, the tribes migrated south and westward, forming settlements and raising cattle and sheep. From the seventh to the ninth centuries, the Khazars, a Turkish tribe, dominated the Magyars. To free themselves from Turkish domination, Magyar tribesmen invaded the lands now known as Hungary around 900 CE.

Many people believe the name *Hungary* is derived from the fact that Huns once occupied the lands. However, other scholars believe the word *Hungary* comes from a Slavicized version of the Turkish words *on ogur*, which mean "ten arrows,"

The ruins of the Dominican convent and church where St. Margaret lived from 1242 to 1271 are still visible on St. Margaret's Island. The island, which is located in the Danube, now is a favorite park for Budapest residents.

For centuries, Hungary was dominated by a feudal system, which saw the creation of large landed estates.

referring to the ten Magyar tribes. According to legend, the tribal chieftains met and chose one among them to rule. They selected a chieftain named Arpad, and swore by drinking from a cup of their commingled blood that they would accept the hereditary rule of Arpad's male descendants—and the Magyar dynasty was established.

By 1001 CE, Hungary was established as a Christian kingdom under Stephen I, a descendant of Arpad. By 1006, Stephen had solidified his power and made sweeping changes to convert Hungary into a **feudal** state. His policies included rapid, forced conversion to Christianity, and the abolishment of traditional **pagan** rites. Stephen created a strong kingdom that was able to withstand invasions from both the east and the west, as well as expanding Hungarian territory by conquering many smaller Slavic kingdoms.

Arpad's descendants ruled until 1301, when a series of military defeats, including a disastrous invasion by the Mongols, led to a weakening of central power and ultimately the rule of monarchs from abroad. Hungarian lands came under control of various foreign monarchs from France, Poland, Luxembourg, and other foreign powers at various times. The situation was highly unstable, and by 1526, a sizable area of Hungary was conquered by the Turks.

By 1541, Hungary was divided into three parts. Present-day Slovakia, Croatia, and northeastern section of modern Hungary came under the rule of the Hapsburg family of Austria as a province known as Royal Hungary. Transylvania became an independent state allied with the Turks. The remaining lands of Hungary, including the twin cities of Buda and Pest (later joined to become the modern capital of Budapest), became a province of the Ottoman Empire. The Hapsburgs conquered Buda again in 1686, and by 1718, all of the original Hungarian territory was under Hapsburg rule.

HAPSBURG RULE

The Hapsburg victory over Turkish forces was followed by strict new measures that ensured the **absolute rule** of the Hapsburg Dynasty and the supremacy of the Roman Catholic Church in the region. All the kingdom of Hungary was declared hereditary property of the Hapsburg family, and all law was issued by royal decree.

In an attempt to rebuild after the losses of the war years, the Hapsburgs pursued a policy of resettlement for their more western holdings. German Catholics immigrated to the area on a large scale and became the new middle class. The entire educational system was placed under Catholic control. German became the dominant language of the region. The Hapsburg policy of **centralization** ultimately took a large toll on the cultures of Central Europe as many of the native languages and cultural practices of the region were wiped out.

By the eighteenth century, Hungary was widely Germanized. During this period, known as the **Age of Enlightenment**, all Europe saw remarkable cultural changes characterized by a loss of faith in traditional religious sources of authority and a turn toward human rights, science, and rational thought. Hapsburg rulers Maria-Theresa and her son Joseph II instituted reforms based on Enlightenment principles to promote social and economic progress.

The consequences of Enlightenment reforms had widespread significance. The power and authority of the Catholic Church was reduced, and some freedom of worship was established. Catholic control of education came to a halt, and the focus of study shifted from theology to the sciences.

By the dawn of the nineteenth century, a great wave of new thinking was sweeping across Central Europe. The aggression of the French general Napoleon Bonaparte created a surge of **nationalism** among Germans. The concept of a nation as a group of people linked by a common language and culture had great appeal to the Magyars who had lived for centuries under foreign rule. Inspired by the renewed interest in German national identity that was taking place among their neighbors, the Hungarian intellectual **elite** soon launched a national revival of their own. As Hungarians became dissatisfied with the refusal of the Hapsburg monarchy to implement reforms that would give more **autonomy** to native Magyars, the stage was set for revolution.

THE REVOLUTION OF 1848

Initially a bloodless revolt centered in the cities of Pest and Buda, the 1848 revolution began on March 15. Mass demonstrations forced imperial administrators to give in to public demands. The success of these demonstrations led to similar revolts erupting across the country. Hungarian revolutionaries declared Hungarian autonomy within the empire and named their own governor and prime minister.

A **civil war** followed, with Magyar forces forced to fight against not only the Austrian Army, but against local forces of Serbs, Croats, Slovaks, Romanians, and ethnic Germans who lived in Hungary and did not support Magyar nationalism. Still, Hungarian forces were initially able to defeat the Austrian troops, partly because the empire's attention was split between the rebellion in Hungary and attempts at revolution at home in Vienna.

By April 1849, Hungarians declared their complete independence from Austria. Seeing that the situation had gotten completely out of control, Austria sought help from their ally, Russia. Czar Nicholas I sent his armies to invade Hungary from the east while Austria renewed their push from the west, and the revolution was subdued. Retribution followed, as did further attempts at Germanization, while the Magyar nationalists pursued **passive** forms of resistance.

The Austro-Hungarian Empire, established in 1867, was a means for the Austrian monarchy to calm political tensions. Austria and Hungary were united as essentially separate governments under one monarch. Foreign policy, military affairs, and the economy were administered centrally, but otherwise Hungary had autonomy over its domestic affairs. The Hungarians united with the Austrians to

Wonderful Baroque architecture, such as the Municipal Baths in the City Park of Budapest, is evidence of the historical importance of Hungary's capital city.

Symbolic Soviet-era statuary looks east over Budapest from the heights of the Citadella,
a fortress built by the Austrians in 1854 to control rebellion in the country.

successfully prevent the region's smaller ethnic minorities, such as the Slovaks, from gaining political power. The new political power wielded by the Magyars was used to implement a wave of reforms to promote Magyar culture after the many years of Germanization Hungary had seen under Austrian rule. Ironically, these measures suppressed the language and cultures of other minorities in the region. The dissatisfaction of the many ethnic groups in Central Europe would eventually lead to World War I.

WORLD WAR I AND THE HUNGARIAN SOCIALIST REPUBLIC

The inability of the Austro-Hungarian Empire to ease tensions between the different nationalities under their rule eventually led to the fall of the empire. World War I began on June 28, 1914, when Gavrilo Princip, a Serbian nationalist, assassinated Austrian archduke Franz Ferdinand and his wife, Sophie. Russia allied with Serbia. Germany sided with Austria and soon declared war on Russia. After France declared its support for Russia, Germany attacked France. German troops then invaded Belgium, a **neutral** country, as it stood between German forces and Paris. Great Britain next declared war on Germany. Eventually defeated, the Austro-Hungarian monarchy collapsed.

After the collapse of the empire, the newly formed nations of Romania, Czechoslovakia, and Yugoslavia made claims to land that had traditionally belonged to Hungary. With the support of the victorious Allied forces, foreign armies occupied much of Hungary. In the face of occupation, and after the fall of a short-lived republic, the **Communist** Party of Hungary came to power. On March 21, 1919, their leader, Bela Kun, proclaimed the creation of the Hungarian Socialist Republic.

Public opinion was split between the Reds who favored communist rule, primarily because the communists had the only organized military force and promised to end foreign occupation, and the Whites who opposed communist rule. Ultimately, the communists were defeated. The chaos that ensued was bloody, with both sides executing members of the opposition without trial. The occupying Romanian army also looted heavily and caused such widespread property damage that Hungary was not required to pay them **war reparations** at the 1919 international peace conference.

As foreign forces withdrew, Whites took power under the leadership of Miklos Horthy, a Transylvanian aristocrat. Horthy's army marched into Budapest on November 16, 1919, and in the weeks that followed, communist activity was suppressed and thousands of communist sympathizers were imprisoned. In a January 1920 election, men and women cast the first secret ballots in the country's history and voted to restore the monarchy under an elected king. Horthy was elected regent and given broad powers, including the power to select a prime minister, dissolve the parliament, and command the armed forces.

Hungary suffered greatly in the years that followed World War I. New borders caused all kinds of problems. Major industries were now separated from traditional sources of raw materials; almost 30 percent of ethnic Magyars found themselves outside the country's new borders. The **Great Depression** of the late 1920s and 1930s further lowered the standard of living and increased political instability in the region. Many of the nation's ills were unfairly blamed on the small Jewish minority, and as Adolf Hitler came to power in nearby Germany, support for his policies became widespread in Hungary.

Nazi Germany and World War II

By 1933, Adolf Hitler had come to power in Germany, and by 1938, he had occupied neighboring Austria as well. His stated objective was to unify all ethnic German peoples. He soon demanded the surrender of Czechoslovakia's Sudetenland, taking up the cause of the Sudeten Germans. On September 29, 1938, France, Germany, Italy, and Great Britain signed the Munich Agreement, demanding that Czechoslovakia surrender the Sudetenland to Germany in exchange for a promise of peace. However, in March 1939, Hitler **reneged** on his agreement and invaded the remainder of Czechoslovakia. The world was once again at war, and Hungary, eager to reclaim the territory it had lost after World War I, allied itself with Nazi Germany.

Attempting to gain favor in the eyes of Nazi officials, Hungary began passing extreme laws aimed at eliminating Hungarian Jews. Initial laws restricted Jews' movement, property ownership, education, and employment, but eventually more than 400,000 Jews were slaughtered. Hungarian forces also participated in the invasion of neighboring Yugoslavia and eventually fought for Germany against the Red Army in Russia. Hungarian losses were heavy, particularly on the Russian front, and Hungary began to conduct secret negotiations with the Allies. Hitler discovered the negotiations and ordered the German army to occupy Hungary.

The Red Army was steadily advancing from Russia. Faced with further defeats on the Western front, the German army had no choice but to retreat. Hungary became a wasteland as retreating Nazi troops destroyed virtually all roads, bridges, and communication systems while looting the countryside for valuables and supplies. In spite of such resistance, the Soviet Red Army eventually prevailed, and the last German troops were driven out on April 4, 1945. It took seven weeks to completely liberate Budapest; in the process, nearly the entire city was destroyed.

A Second Communist Government

Once again, Hungary had suffered a massive military defeat, and now under Soviet occupation, the nation watched its fate unfold at the peace table. The international community offered no support for any measure to change Hungary's 1938 borders. Hungary was forced to surrender all the land it had acquired during the war, and the Soviet Union annexed the region known as Sub-Carpathia,

ECO SUM VIA VERITAS ET VITA

St. Stephen's Basilica in Budapest is a symbol of the grandeur of the Hungarian nation.
The church keeps the right hand of St. Stephen as a relic in an interior chapel.

The neo-Gothic Hungarian Parliament building, located on the Pest side of the Danube River, was constructed in 1904. The statues nearby attest to the military struggles that the Hungarian land has seen.

which is now a part of the modern nation of Ukraine. With the political situation strongly influenced by the occupying Red Army, it was only a matter of time before communism took hold. Thousands were executed and imprisoned during various struggles for power between different personalities within the Communist Party.

By 1956, there was widespread dissatisfaction with the communist regime. The Hungarian uprising began on October 23, 1956, as a peaceful student demonstration in Budapest. Police tried to disrupt the demonstration by releasing tear gas on the crowd. As students attempted to help those who were injured or detained, police opened fire on the crowd. The following day, soldiers joined students in the crowd and brought down a statue of Stalin. On October 25, Soviet tanks moved in and opened fire on protesters.

The harsh reprisals led to the formation of a coalition government. Hungary requested assistance from the United Nations in settling its dispute with the Soviet Union. Alarmed at these developments, Soviet leader Nikita Khrushchev ordered the Red Army into Hungary. In the ensuing fighting, an estimated 20,000 people were killed. The Soviets installed a Soviet loyalist, Janos Kadar, as secretary general of the Communist Party.

At the outset, Kadar's government led a great purge against revolutionaries, imprisoning and executing thousands. As the years passed, however, Kadar eventually gave in to pressure for political and economic reform. By 1980, there had been some economic liberalization, and by 1988, Kadar was replaced, and the parliament passed a "democracy package." This legislation included a number of **radical** reform measures, including **privatization** of businesses; freedoms of association, assembly, and the press; democratic reforms in the electoral laws; and a dramatic revision of the constitution.

THE ROAD AHEAD

Among the communist countries of the former Soviet **bloc**, Hungary's transition to a Western-style democracy was not only one of the earliest, but also one of the smoothest. Political reforms have led to a modern democracy, and economic reforms have helped Hungary to reach out to trading partners in the West. Now emerging from a period of economic **recession**, Hungary is investing in reform of the pension system, **infrastructure**, health care, and higher education. As a new member of the EU, Hungary is prepared to play a significant role in the development and growth of Central Europe.

The Buda district of Budapest makes an impressive sight day or night with hills topped by forts and churches.

3 THE ECONOMY

After a stormy history, Hungarians are finally able to regard their economic future with optimism. Although Hungary began to liberalize its economy under communism, long before many of the other Soviet bloc countries, the initial hopes for a rapid rise in the standard of living were not realized. Instead, Hungary faced a host of financial woes following the end of communism.

The Danube River is a conduit for commerce and tourism. Thousands of visitors annually cruise its waters on large riverboats.

An Economy in Distress

Following the dismantling of the communist system in the late 1980s, Hungary planned to pursue the development of a stable **market economy**, eventually leading to greater growth and foreign investment.

Unfortunately, reform was slow in taking hold, and foreign investment was weak due to the perceived instability of the area. By the mid-1990s, unemployment had soared as high as 14 percent, inflation ballooned to 35 percent, and the forint (the Hungarian monetary unit) had lost more than half its value between 1992 and 1996.

Building a New Economy

With all economic indicators on the decline and basic necessities such as food, medicine, transportation, and energy rising in cost, the outlook for the Hungarian economy was not good. It became clear that there was no way for current levels of domestic production to support the needed overhaul of Hungarian industry. Not only would Hungary require foreign funds to help update an antiquated infrastructure, but new technology, business methods, and management strategies were needed as well.

Quick Facts: The Economy of Hungary

Gross Domestic Product (GDP): US$139.8 billion

GDP per capita: US$13,900

Industries: mining, metallurgy, construction materials, processed foods, textiles, chemicals, motor vehicles

Agriculture: wheat, corn, sunflower seed, potatoes, sugar beet; pigs, cattle, poultry, dairy products

Export commodities: machinery and equipment, other manufactures, food products, raw materials, fuels and electricity

Export partners: Germany 34.1%, Austria 8%, Italy 5.8%, France 5.7%, UK 4.5%, Netherlands 4.1% (2003)

Import commodities: machinery and equipment, other manufactures, fuels and electricity, food products, raw materials

Import partners: Germany 24.5%, Italy 7.1%, China 6.9%, Austria 6.3%, Russia 6.2%, France 4.8%, Japan 4.2% (2003)

Currency: forint (HUF)

Currency exchange rate: US$1 = 183.520 HUF (December 16, 2004)

Note: All figures are from 2004 unless otherwise noted.
Source: www.cia.gov, 2005.

Today, Hungary has emerged from the transition period of the 1990s as a robust, fully functioning market economy. It receives more than 90 percent of capital from foreign companies investing in the region. By highlighting the availability of a skilled labor force at a relatively low wage, Hungary has managed to lure companies from other parts of Europe, North America, and Asia.

Unemployment has dropped dramatically in most of the country, although northern Hungary still remains economically disadvantaged. This influx of foreign money helped pave the way for modernization that was critical to Hungary's admission to the EU. As a result of these reforms, Hungary is now one of Europe's fastest-growing and most open economies, deeply integrated into the larger European economy.

MANUFACTURING: THE MAINSTAY OF THE ECONOMY AND EXPORTS

Heavy industry is an important part of Hungary's economy. The ultimate success of the Hungarian economy is dependent on the export of motor vehicles, electronics, and chemicals.

The electronic machine and instrument category comprises the manufacture of telecommunications devices, and electronic consumer goods (TV sets, videocassette recorders, radio receivers, and CD players), other parts (semiconductors, resistors, condensers, electromechanical parts), and components. The manufacture of consumer electronics accounted for almost 40 percent of Hungary's exports.

Another important and fast-growing branch of Hungary's manufacturing sector is the automobile industry. Twenty-four percent of all Hungarian exports are accounted for by the vehicle manufacturing industry in Hungary. Two important sectors of this industry are motor vehicle assembly and automotive-parts manufacturing. Due to the arrival of multinational companies in the car and automotive-parts industries in Hungary and their large-scale investments in plants and equipment, the Hungarian automotive industry has developed rapidly to achieve the world-class level necessary to serve the greater European market. Hungary has experienced especially explosive growth in the manufacture of electric parts for vehicles.

Major automotive companies, including General Motors, Audi, Suzuki, and Lear Automotive, have established multimillion dollar investments for auto-assembly and parts manufacture. Hungary was able to offer these companies important advantages including skilled, low-wage labor; an ever-increasing automotive supplier and vendor network; a stable economy; and a highly advantageous location in Central Europe. These companies are expanding operations and manufacturing and are seeking to use more Hungarian components. The Hungarian government has targeted increased investment in this sector as a primary goal.

Food processing, chemicals, and pharmaceuticals are also vital industries in the new Hungarian economy.

The limestone hills surrounding Lake Balaton are where some of Hungary's best wine grapes are grown.

AGRICULTURE

Despite thousands of acres of open farmland, Hungary is predominantly an industrial society. Farming brings in only 8 percent of the **_gross domestic product (GDP)_** and caters mainly to local needs rather than to export. Crops produced include wheat, corn, sunflower seeds, potatoes, fruit, and sugar beets. Pigs, cattle, poultry, and dairy products are also produced. EU accession is hoped to bring in additional funds to support Hungarian agriculture, as the EU's Common Agricultural Policy (CAP) heavily subsidizes Hungary's farming sector.

Energy Sources

The rapid growth of industry in Hungary has created larger demands for energy. Domestic energy production from oil, gas, nuclear power, and coal meets approximately half of Hungary's current energy requirements. Additional energy needs are met from imported oil and natural gas. Since domestic energy production has peaked, when energy consumption begins to rise, dependency on foreign imports will probably also increase. The Hungarian government has developed a new energy policy to research new energy sources and eliminate dependency on foreign imports, improve environmental protection, and secure foreign funds for investment in new energy projects.

Millions of Budapest's residents depend on Budapest's efficient trains and buses, which relieve congestion in the crowded downtown.

TRANSPORTATION

The Hungarian transportation system is currently undergoing a major reconstruction to build a large network of four-lane highways, which currently only cover a small portion of the country. The government-controlled domestic railway system is widely used for industrial shipping due to its low cost and high reliability. The nation's waterways also provide important commercial transport.

Hungary's major international airport is located in Budapest and currently operates from two modern terminals. Budapest is serviced by numerous major international airlines, as well as charter service to smaller cities in the region. Regular domestic air service connects the capital of Budapest with Miskolc, a major industrial city in eastern Hungary, which has helped to assist the further economic growth of this part of Hungary. Larger cities maintain airports for private aircraft, and the govern-ment plans to transform several former Soviet military air bases into domestic passenger and cargo airfields.

A GROWING CENTER FOR TRADE

In addition to the success Hungary has had in marketing itself to foreign companies as a home for manufacturing, foreign investment has focused on the unique position of Hungary as a center for trade. Historically, Hungary has been a cross-roads for trade in Europe. Today, with the prosperous EU to the west and economically developing nations to the south and east, Hungary offers not only an export market, but a useful distribution point for the entire region.

GETTING BACK ON ITS FEET

The many years of investment and reform since the end of communism are finally beginning to pay off for the Hungarian people. As Hungary looks to the future, indications are good that the Hungarian people will eventually share the same prosperity, security, and standard of living that citizens of other, more established EU member nations enjoy.

Budapest's public transit system includes Europe's oldest section of underground railroad, which opened in 1896.

4 HUNGARY'S PEOPLE AND CULTURE

Nearly two-thirds of Hungary's population live in urban areas, but the majority of towns in Hungary have populations of less than 40,000. They were, until very recently, over-grown villages rather than modern towns. Almost one-third of Hungary's urban population lives within the Budapest metropolitan area.

More than 90 percent of the population is ethnically Hungarian and speaks Hungarian (Magyar) as its mother tongue. About 3 percent of the population is Roma or Gypsy, and nearly another 5 percent is made up of Slovaks, Romanians, Croats, Germans, and others. The Hungarian language is classified as a member of the Ugric branch of the Uralic languages. This language is distantly related to Finnish and Estonian.

QUICK FACTS: THE PEOPLE OF HUNGARY

Population: 10,032,375 (July 2004 est.)

Ethnic groups: Hungarian 89.9%, Roma 4%, German 2.6%, Serb 2%, Slovak 0.8%, Romanian 0.7%

Age structure:
   0–14 years: 16%
   15–64 years: 69%
   65 years and over: 15%

Population growth rate: –0.25%

Birth rate: 9.77 births/1,000 pop.

Death rate: 13.16 deaths/1,000 pop.

Migration rate: 0.86 migrant(s)/1,000 pop.

Infant mortality rate: 8.68 deaths/1,000 live births

Life expectancy at birth:
   Total population: 72.25 years
   Males: 68.07 years
   Females: 76.69 years

Total fertility rate: 1.31 children born/woman

Religions: Roman Catholic 67.5%, Calvinist 20%, Lutheran 5%, atheist and other 7.5%

Languages: Hungarian 98.2%, other 1.8%

Literacy rate: 99.4%

Note: All figures are from 2004 unless noted.
Source: www.cia.gov, 2005.

RELIGION: FREEDOM OF CHOICE

The Hungarian constitution guarantees freedom of conscience and religion. Currently, about 67 percent of the population is Roman Catholic, 20 percent is Reformed (Calvinist), 5 percent are unaffiliated, and 5 percent are Lutheran. Other Christian denominations include Uniates, Orthodox, and various small Protestant groups, such as Baptists, Methodists, Seventh-Day Adventists, and Mormons. Most of these smaller groups are affiliated with the national Council of Free Churches and are dubbed the "free churches" as a group. The country is also estimated to have 65,000 to 100,000 practicing Jews.

FOOD AND DRINK

Hungary's unique cuisine has been shaped not only by the traditional dishes of the Magyars, but by influences from the Turks, Germans, French, Austrians, Czechs, Slovaks, Serbians, and Croatians.

Hearty Hungarian fare relies on sauces rich in sour cream. High-calorie

St. Stephen, who was crowned on Christmas Day 1000, is revered for Christianizing Hungary.
His statue stands behind the Mathias Church in the Buda section of the capital.

Schoolchildren in Hungary are experiencing firsthand profound reforms in the educational system.

EUROPEAN UNION—HUNGARY

delicacies such as goose liver and meats, including game such as boar and venison, are often on the menu. Eel stew and a thick and sometimes peppery fish soup are popular national dishes. Perhaps the most famous Hungarian dish is goulash, a type of beef stew that has gained popularity in the West. Other traditional favorites include veal paprika stew and roast chicken with cottage cheese noodles. Desserts, typically served with strong espresso, include strudels, tortes, and pancakes topped with chocolate rum sauce. Modern lifestyles have brought some changes in Hungarian eating habits. Chefs in the larger cities are preparing lighter versions of traditional favorites and focusing on leaner meats.

As for beverages, Hungarians are proud of their domestically produced wines. Hungary boasts twenty wine-producing districts, which make a wide range of wines, including cabernet sauvignon, pinot gris, merlot, riesling, chardonnay, and traditional Hungarian varieties such as the sweet white tokaji aszu and the strong red bull's blood.

EDUCATION: A TIME OF GREAT CHANGE

Education in Hungary has undergone historic reforms in recent years. No other country in Central Europe has approached the reform of the public school system in quite the same manner. Under central planning, the Hungarian school system was highly **regimented** and focused toward either vocational and technical training or preparation for university study. Schools adhered strictly to a national curriculum, with no adjustments made for the specific needs of the communities the schools served.

Under the new education system, responsibility for the administration of schools was given directly to the local community, along with the power to control education in many ways. A number of private and church-affiliated schools have been established. Schools now operate outside the old definitions of primary and secondary schools, and the curriculum may vary greatly from one area to the next. Focus has also shifted somewhat from pursuit of vocational training to exposing all students to more rigorous academic courses. Time will tell what impact this community-driven model of education will have on the future Hungarian workforce.

SPORTS AND LEISURE: A FUN-LOVING PEOPLE

Hungarians are known for their love of the outdoors, reflected in their long-standing tradition of horsemanship and the popularity of water sports. Swimming, rowing, fishing, cycling, hiking, and horseback riding are all popular pastimes. Hungarians are also devoted sports fans, and favorite national sports include ice hockey, soccer (known as football), and tennis.

Adventure sports are also becoming more popular in Hungary, with river rafting, caving, and activities like bungee jumping gaining enthusiasts among tourists and native Hungarians alike.

In certain regions, hunting and bird watching are favorite pastimes as well.

ARTS AND ARCHITECTURE

Nowhere is Hungary's history as a crossroads of European and Asian cultures more easily appreciated than when admiring the country's wide vari-

Despite their embrace of modern technology, Hungarians also actively maintain their cultural heritage of music and dance.

ety of architecture. Celtic and Roman ruins can be found in the ancient streets of Buda; medieval castles, Turkish baths, and Renaissance cathedrals are within a short distance from each other. Europe's largest synagogue can be found in Budapest, a stunning example of Byzantine design.

The country also boasts a score of museums, showcasing works of art from every conceivable

style and period. The Vasarely Museum has a formidable collection of works by Victor Vasarely, the Pecs native who pioneered **op art**. Outside the Modern Hungarian Art Gallery, stand the striking sculptures of Pierre Szekely. Inside, are works by important nineteenth- and twentieth-century Hungarian painters. Other museums highlight **abstract** and **surrealist** art. Whatever visitors' artistic tastes, there is sure to be at least one venue to attract their attention.

MUSIC: A RICH HERITAGE

The performances of musicians and minstrels are recorded as entertaining kings of the House of Árpád early in Magyar history. Later on, court music was as much a part of the Gothic way of life in Hungary as it was anywhere else in Europe. Hungarians continue to enjoy a wide diversity of music today, while concerts across the country celebrate the accomplishments of famous Hungarian composers, and also expose Hungarian audiences to new types of music from around the world.

Many Hungarian composers have achieved international fame. Austrian-born Joseph Haydn lived and composed from 1761 to 1790 in the Esterhazy Palace in Fertod. The celebrated composer and pianist Franz Liszt (1811–1886), who for a long time lived abroad, contributed significantly to the development of Hungarian music. Today, conductors, orchestras, and musicians from all over the world come to Hungary to give guest performances in Budapest's two opera houses, at the Academy of Music, and in concert halls. Budapest has become a cultural center for the entire country.

Budapest spans both sides of the Danube River, a conduit for commerce and industry.

5 CHAPTER THE CITIES

Most Hungarians today live in small or medium-sized cities that evolved over time from the small feudal villages of the past. Nearly one-third of the urban population lives in the area surrounding Budapest. The remaining cities retain the charm of centuries past by virtue of their rich history and small populations.

BUDAPEST: THE CAPITAL

Budapest is Hungary's capital and most populated city. The sixth-largest city in the EU, Budapest is the nation's political, industrial, and commercial center. An ancient city, recorded settlement goes back as far as 89 CE, when the Roman town of Aquincum was founded on the ruins of an old Celtic settlement. Over time, twin cities of Buda and Pest developed on opposite sides of the Danube River, and ultimately they joined in 1873 to become the modern city of Budapest.

Owing in part to its advantageous location on the Danube River, Budapest has always been a hub for trade and transportation. Today it is home to the country's only international airport and is an important commercial port. Budapest is also rich in cultural attractions and its many museums, art galleries, and music venues make it a major tourist destination.

DEBRECEN: A CITY ON THE GREAT PLAIN

Hungary's second-most populated city, Debrecen is a center for culture, commerce, and science. The city has developed rapidly in recent years owing to a large influx of foreign investment. Located on the Great Hungarian Plain, the city is relatively isolated, although improvements to Hungary's highway and rail systems should help alleviate that problem. The Debrecen airport has also undergone an important renovation to enable it to accommodate international flights. Debrecen is also home to a large university.

MISKOLC: A CITY OF HISTORY

Inhabited since ancient times, the city of Miskolc was originally settled by the Celts. Various tribal groups took over until the city was conquered by the Magyars in the late ninth century. In later centuries, Turkish forces occupied the city. These different cultures have left their mark on Miskolc, the primary center of northeastern Hungary.

A major center for industry during the communist years, Miskolc suffered during the economic downturn of the 1990s. Population in the city has declined since the fall of communism, and commerce has suffered. The leaders of Miskolc are now trying to capitalize on their city's rich history by promoting the area as a tourist destination and cultural center. The city boasts a great deal of significant architecture, including an enormous Gothic fortress. Miskolc also hosts several important cultural festivals, the most prominent of which is the International Opera Festival, held every summer.

PECS: A CULTURAL HUB

Another Hungarian city that has been frequently occupied since ancient times, Pecs is a treasure of antiquities. Located in southwest Hungary, archaeological finds have been made in Pecs that are more than six thousand years old. Visitors can see remnants of the later Roman occupants of the city and marvel at the many early Christian cemeteries and cathedrals.

Pecs is also filled with opportunities to enjoy the arts. Museums are scattered throughout the city, and concerts and cultural festivals can be enjoyed

Many of Budapest's cultural and historical monuments are located on the hilly Buda side of the city.

Tourists from all over the world visit Budapest, which is known for its fine dining, as well as its museums and churches.

year round. Pecs is becoming a popular destination for tourists and has benefited greatly from the increase in foreign tourism that Hungary has seen since the fall of communism.

Gyor: A City of Diverse Influences

Gyor's history reflects the turmoil of Hungarian history itself. Founded by the Celts, this city in northwest Hungary has been occupied at times by virtually every group to inhabit Hungary. Romans were displaced by Slavs, who were driven out by the Lombards. Next the city fell under control of the Avars, and then the Franks, until the Magyars moved in around 900. It was later invaded and conquered by the Mongols, and then briefly occupied by the Czech Army before reverting to Magyar control. Next, the Ottomans moved in, but were eventually driven back as the city returned to Hungarian control. The city's main fortress was even occupied by Napoleon at one point. It is no coincidence that the name Gyor comes from a Turkish word meaning "burnt city."

Despite centuries of turmoil, the Gyor of today is a thriving university town. Not surprisingly, the city has also developed a bustling tourist industry as people come from all over to see the many different examples of art and architecture left from the city's ancient and chaotic past. Recently, Gyor won a European award for historic preservation and monument protection.

Hungary's cities boast a variety of cultural and historical treasures. Each in their own way contribute to their nation's modern role in the EU.

The EU flag

6

THE FORMATION OF THE EUROPEAN UNION

The EU is an economic and political confederation of twenty-five European nations. Member countries abide by common foreign and security policies and cooperate on judicial and domestic affairs. The confederation, however, does not replace existing states or governments. Each of the twenty-five member states is *autonomous*, but they have all agreed to establish some common institutions and to hand over some of their own decision-making powers to these international bodies. As a result, decisions on matters that interest all member states can be made democratically, accommodating everyone's concerns and interests.

Today, the EU is the most powerful regional organization in the world. It has evolved from a primarily economic organization to an increasingly political one. Besides promoting economic cooperation, the EU requires that its members uphold fundamental values of peace and **solidarity**, human dignity, freedom, and equality. Based on the principles of democracy and the rule of law, the EU respects the culture and organizations of member states.

History

The seeds of the EU were planted more than fifty years ago in a Europe reduced to smoking piles of rubble by two world wars. European nations suffered great financial difficulties in the postwar period. They were struggling to get back on their feet and realized that another war would cause further hardship. Knowing that internal conflict was hurting all of Europe, a drive began toward European cooperation.

France took the first historic step. On May 9, 1950 (now celebrated as Europe Day), Robert Schuman, the French foreign minister, proposed the coal and steel industries of France and West Germany be coordinated under a single supranational authority. The proposal, known as the Treaty

of Paris, attracted four other countries—Belgium, Luxembourg, the Netherlands, and Italy—and resulted in the 1951 formation of the European Coal and Steel Community (ECSC). These six countries became the founding members of the EU.

In 1957, European cooperation took its next big leap. Under the Treaty of Rome, the European Economic Community (EEC) and the European Atomic Energy Community (EURATOM) were formed. Informally known as the Common Market, the EEC promoted joining the national economies into a single European economy. The 1965 Treaty of Brussels (more commonly referred to as the Merger Treaty) united these various treaty organizations under a single umbrella, the European Community (EC).

In 1992, the Maastricht Treaty (also known as the Treaty of the European Union) was signed in Maastricht, the Netherlands, signaling the birth of the EU as it stands today. **Ratified** the following year, the Maastricht Treaty provided for a central banking system, a common currency (the euro) to replace the national currencies, a legal definition of the EU, and a framework for expanding the

The EU's united economy has allowed it to become a worldwide financial power.

EU's political role, particularly in the area of foreign and security policy.

By 1993, the member countries completed their move toward a single market and agreed to participate in a larger common market, the European Economic Area, established in 1994.

The EU, headquartered in Brussels, Belgium, reached its current member strength in spurts. In

© BCE ECB EZB EKT EKP 2002

© BCE ECB EZB EKT EKP 2002

© BCE ECB EZB EKT EKP 2002

© BCE ECB EZB EKT EKP 2002

The euro, the EU's currency

1973, Denmark, Ireland, and the United Kingdom joined the six founding members of the EC. They were followed by Greece in 1981, and Portugal and Spain in 1986. The 1990s saw the unification of the two Germanys, and as a result, East Germany entered the EU fold. Austria, Finland, and Sweden joined the EU in 1995, bringing the total number of member states to fifteen. In 2004, the EU nearly doubled its size when ten countries—Cyprus, the Czech Republic, Estonia, Hungary, Latvia, Lithuania, Malta, Poland, Slovakia, and Slovenia—became members.

THE EU FRAMEWORK

The EU's structure has often been compared to a "roof of a temple with three columns." As established by the Maastricht Treaty, this three-pillar framework encompasses all the policy areas—or pillars—of European cooperation. The three pillars of the EU are the European Community, the Common Foreign and Security Policy (CFSP), and Police and Judicial Co-operation in Criminal Matters.

QUICK FACTS: THE EUROPEAN UNION

Number of Member Countries: 25
Official Languages: 20—Czech, Danish, Dutch, English, Estonian, Finnish, French, German, Greek, Hungarian, Italian, Latvian, Lithuanian, Maltese, Polish, Portuguese, Slovak, Slovenian, Spanish, and Swedish; additional language for treaty purposes: Irish Gaelic.
Motto: *In Varietate Concordia* (United in Diversity)
European Council's President: Each member state takes a turn to lead the council's activities for 6 months
European Commission's President: José Manuel Barroso (Portugal)
European Parliament's President: Josep Borrell (Spain)
Total Area: 1,502,966 square miles (3,892,685 sq. km.)
Population: 454,900,000
Population Density: 302.7 people/square mile (116.8 people/sq. km.)
GDP: €9.61.1012
Per Capita GDP: €21,125
Formation:
- Declared: February 7, 1992, with signing of the Maastricht Treaty
- Recognized: November 1, 1993, with the ratification of the Maastricht Treaty

Community Currency: Euro. Currently 12 of the 25 member states have adopted the euro as their currency.
Anthem: "Ode to Joy"
Flag: Blue background with 12 gold stars arranged in a circle
Official Day: Europe Day, May 9

Source: europa.eu.int

PILLAR ONE

The European Community pillar deals with economic, social, and environmental policies. It is a body consisting of the European Parliament, European Commission, European Court of Justice, Council of the European Union, and the European Courts of Auditors.

PILLAR TWO

The idea that the EU should speak with one voice in world affairs is as old as the European integration process itself. Toward this end, the Common Foreign and Security Policy (CFSP) was formed in 1993.

PILLAR THREE

The cooperation of EU member states in judicial and criminal matters ensures that its citizens enjoy the freedom to travel, work, and live securely and safely anywhere within the EU. The third pillar—Police and Judicial Co-operation in Criminal Matters—helps to protect EU citizens from international crime and to ensure equal access to justice and fundamental rights across the EU.

The flags of the EU's nations:

top row, left to right
Belgium, the Czech Republic, Denmark, Germany, Estonia, Greece

second row, left to right
Spain, France, Ireland, Italy, Cyprus, Latvia

third row, left to right
Lithuania, Luxembourg, Hungary, Malta, the Netherlands, Austria

bottom row, left to right
Poland, Portugal, Slovenia, Slovakia, Finland, Sweden, United Kingdom

ECONOMIC STATUS

As of May 2004, the EU had the largest economy in the world, followed closely by the United States. But even though the EU continues to enjoy a trade surplus, it faces the twin problems of high unemployment rates and **stagnancy**.

The 2004 addition of ten new member states is expected to boost economic growth. EU membership is likely to stimulate the economies of these relatively poor countries. In turn, their prosperity growth will be beneficial to the EU.

THE EURO

The EU's official currency is the euro, which came into circulation on January 1, 2002. The shift to the euro has been the largest monetary changeover in the world. Twelve countries—Belgium, Germany, Greece, Spain, France, Ireland, Italy, Luxembourg, the Netherlands, Finland, Portugal, and Austria—have adopted it as their currency.

SINGLE MARKET

Within the EU, laws of member states are harmonized and domestic policies are coordinated to create a larger, more-efficient single market.

The chief features of the EU's internal policy on the single market are:

- free trade of goods and services

- a common EU competition law that controls anticompetitive activities of companies and member states

- removal of internal border control and harmonization of external controls between member states

- freedom for citizens to live and work anywhere in the EU as long as they are not dependent on the state

- free movement of **capital** between member states

- harmonization of government regulations, corporation law, and trademark registration

- a single currency

- coordination of environmental policy

- a common agricultural policy and a common fisheries policy

- a common system of indirect taxation, the value-added tax (VAT), and common customs duties and **excise**

- funding for research

- funding for aid to disadvantaged regions

The EU's external policy on the single market specifies:

- a common external **tariff** and a common position in international trade negotiations

- funding of programs in other Eastern European countries and developing countries

COOPERATION AREAS

EU member states cooperate in other areas as well. Member states can vote in European Parliament elections. Intelligence sharing and cooperation in criminal matters are carried out through EUROPOL and the Schengen Information System.

The EU is working to develop common foreign and security policies. Many member states are resisting such a move, however, saying these are sensitive areas best left to individual member states. Arguing in favor of a common approach to security and foreign policy are countries like France and Germany, who insist that a safer and more secure Europe can only become a reality under the EU umbrella.

One of the EU's great achievements has been to create a boundary-free area within which people, goods, services, and money can move around freely; this ease of movement is sometimes called "the four freedoms." As the EU grows in size, so do the challenges facing it—and yet its fifty-year history has amply demonstrated the power of cooperation.

Europe is proud of its "bright idea," a union with economic and political power.

The EU believes that it can use its power to act as a "lighthouse" for the rest of the world.

KEY EU INSTITUTIONS

Five key institutions play a specific role in the EU.

THE EUROPEAN PARLIAMENT

The European Parliament (EP) is the democratic voice of the people of Europe. Directly elected every five years, the Members of the European Parliament (MEPs) sit not in national blocs but in political groups representing the seven main political parties of the member states. Each group reflects the political ideology of the national parties to which its members belong. Some MEPs are not attached to any political group.

COUNCIL OF THE EUROPEAN UNION

The Council of the European Union (formerly known as the Council of Ministers) is the main leg-

islative and decision-making body in the EU. It brings together the nationally elected representatives of the member-state governments. One minister from each of the EU's member states attends council meetings. It is the forum in which government representatives can assert their interests and reach compromises. Increasingly, the Council of the European Union and the EP are acting together as colegislators in decision-making processes.

EUROPEAN COMMISSION

The European Commission does much of the day-to-day work of the EU. Politically independent, the commission represents the interests of the EU as a whole, rather than those of individual member states. It drafts proposals for new European laws, which it presents to the EP and the Council of the European Union. The European Commission makes sure EU decisions are implemented properly and supervises the way EU funds are spent. It also sees that everyone abides by the European treaties and European law.

The EU member-state governments choose the European Commission president, who is then approved by the EP. Member states, in consultation with the incoming president, nominate the other European Commission members, who must also be approved by the EP. The commission is appointed for a five-year term, but can be dismissed by the EP. Many members of its staff work in Brussels, Belgium.

COURT OF JUSTICE

Headquartered in Luxembourg, the Court of Justice of the European Communities consists of one independent judge from each EU country. This court ensures that the common rules decided in the EU are understood and followed uniformly by all the members. The Court of Justice settles disputes over how EU treaties and legislation are interpreted. If national courts are in doubt about how to apply EU rules, they must ask the Court of Justice. Individuals can also bring proceedings against EU institutions before the court.

COURT OF AUDITORS

EU funds must be used legally, economically, and for their intended purpose. The Court of Auditors, an independent EU institution located in Luxembourg, is responsible for overseeing how EU money is spent. In effect, these auditors help European taxpayers get better value for the money that has been channeled into the EU.

OTHER IMPORTANT BODIES

1. European Economic and Social Committee: expresses the opinions of organized civil society on economic and social issues

2. Committee of the Regions: expresses the opinions of regional and local authorities

3. European Central Bank: responsible for monetary policy and managing the euro

4. European Ombudsman: deals with citizens' complaints about mismanagement by any EU institution or body

5. European Investment Bank: helps achieve EU objectives by financing investment projects

Together with a number of agencies and other bodies completing the system, the EU's institutions have made it the most powerful organization in the world.

EU Member States

In order to become a member of the EU, a country must have a stable democracy that guarantees the rule of law, human rights, and protection of minorities. It must also have a functioning market economy as well as a civil service capable of applying and managing EU laws.

The EU provides substantial financial assistance and advice to help candidate countries prepare themselves for membership. As of October 2004, the EU has twenty-five member states. Bulgaria and Romania are likely to join in 2007, which would bring the EU's total population to nearly 500 million.

In December 2004, the EU decided to open negotiations with Turkey on its proposed membership. Turkey's possible entry into the EU has been fraught with controversy. Much of this controversy has centered on Turkey's human rights record and the divided island of Cyprus. If allowed to join the EU, Turkey would be its most-populous member state.

The 2004 expansion was the EU's most ambitious enlargement to date. Never before has the EU embraced so many new countries, grown so much in terms of area and population, or encompassed so many different histories and cultures. As the EU moves forward into the twenty-first century, it will undoubtedly continue to grow in both political and economic strength.

From the Esztergom Cathedral, the largest church in Hungary, you can see the miles of rolling hills in the northern section of the country.

7 HUNGARY IN THE EUROPEAN UNION

Ten new member nations were admitted to the EU in 2004. These nations were Hungary, Cyprus, Estonia, Slovakia, Latvia, Lithuania, Malta, Poland, the Czech Republic, and Slovenia. As a relatively new member of the EU, Hungary is looking forward to new opportunities as it adjusts to the new economic and political situation.

A Return to Europe

Hungary was the first of the former Soviet bloc nations to seek membership in the EU. Through EU membership, Hungary hopes to achieve increased security as well as political and economic stability. Although Hungary has emerged as a stable democracy, many of its neighbors, particularly in the Balkan region, have had much more turbulent transitions from communist rule—and foreign investment depends to a large extent on the perception of not only a country but the region. It became clear in the early 1990s that Hungary needed to more closely identify itself with the established powers in Europe in order to reassure potential investors that Hungary was a stable and safe place to conduct business.

The need for a greater identification with Europe is also rooted in Hungarian political policies. Hungarians have considered themselves to be Europeans ever since the first kingdom of Hungary was established under Stephen I. Due to forces outside the control of the average Hungarian citizen, Hungary was cut off from its historical ties in the West following the communist takeover that followed World War II. The Hungarian people today believe that Hungary belongs united with the rest of Europe.

Differing Views of a United Europe

Despite this trend, public opinion in Europe remains divided about the amount of decision-making control member nations should surrender to the EU. Most Hungarians want to surrender a minimum of **sovereignty**, especially over such things as defense and foreign policy. Concern has been expressed that as a nation that has only recently gained a democratically elected legislative body, the Hungarian voting public should have more control over legislation being passed than the European Parliament in Brussels.

Currently, Hungary and many of the other new EU states support a policy termed intergovernmentalism—a governmental approach in which member states must decide on policy by unanimous agreement. Hungary remains concerned that their status as a new member of the EU and their relative economic weakness puts their interests behind the interests of larger countries like Germany in EU decision making. This feeling has been fueled by a controversy over Hungarian representation in the European Parliament.

Hungary was awarded twenty seats in the European Parliament in Brussels. The parliament drafts legislation to be followed by all twenty-six member states of the EU. Hungary has protested their allotment of only twenty delegates, when based on their population, they should have been awarded

twenty-two; other nations of the same size, such as Greece, have twenty-two delegates. Hungary's citizens feel that their limited seats in parliament reflects their relative weakness as an EU member, compared to more prosperous countries.

Others nations, primarily in the larger EU countries such as Germany, do not share Hungary's view. They feel strongly that the great-est opportunities for growth can be found within the framework of a strongly united Europe. Supporters of supranationalism—a governmental approach in which EU member states would be bound by decisions based on majority rule—believe that the benefits of having common policies for defense, treaty negotiation, and trade far out-weigh the individual interests of separate member

The children of Hungary are taught about its proud heritage.
Many Hungarians are reluctant to surrender substantial sovereignty as a cost of joining the European Union.

states. They also point to the economic burdens they face in supporting the smaller, less economically developed nations of the union while they work toward a full and equal partnership.

BENEFITS OF EU MEMBERSHIP

EU membership is expected to have a positive impact on the standard of living in many parts of Hungary. Many reforms were made in order for Hungary to be eligible for EU membership, but a great deal of work remains.

For example, great discrepancies exist between the standard of living enjoyed by urban Hungarians and the conditions faced by poorer Hungarians in the more rural northern areas of the country. Only four major highways are completely functional. Many other highways are being built,

Two of Hungary's most famous agricultural products are paprika and fine wines, both of which are for sale at this roadside shop in the town of Tihany.

and Hungary is depending on EU funds to assist with that construction.

As a new member of the EU, Hungary will be able to access millions of dollars in additional funding provided to develop an infrastructure that is comparable to the rest of Europe. The funds are allocated to help address the economic and social inequalities between the richest and poorest EU nations. This money will be used to support agriculture, build new roads and bridges, improve health-care and social welfare programs, and improve environmental conditions. All these improvements are designed to promote continued foreign investment.

With the financial assistance Hungary receives from the EU helping to create a favorable business environment, Hungarians are able to lower their own corporate taxes in hope of luring companies away from areas where it is more expensive to do business. The potential of economic assistance to help level the playing field between Hungary and its neighbors to the west was one of the strongest motivating factors behind the decision to move forward with EU accession.

Although agriculture is not a major industry in Hungary, it is an active supporter of the EU's CAP.

The program's aim is to provide farmers with a decent standard of living and consumers across Europe with safe and fresh food at reasonable prices. Hungary is hopeful that the owners of its small farms will be able to access subsidies that will help to develop new farming practices. This is important, since environmental concerns about land use and the safety of Europe's food supply have attracted public attention.

To be eligible for EU assistance, Hungarian farmers will have to uphold high standards of quality. Additionally, they will have to comply with new legislation dealing with the environment, animal welfare, hygiene standards, and preservation of the countryside. It is hoped that additional funding for farmers will spur increased economic growth in the areas of agriculture and related industries, such as food processing.

LOOKING FORWARD

While a few concerns over their sovereignty and national interests persist, there is little doubt that the EU will greatly improve the standard of living, economic security, and prominence of Hungary on the world stage. The availability of EU funds for building a more stable infrastructure and a favorable climate for foreign investment is helping to maintain a steady recovery from the poverty that marked the nation's years as a communist state. It seems clear that EU membership will aid Hungary in successfully establishing its place as a major political and economic force in Europe.

A Calendar of Hungarian Festivals

Hungary celebrates many religious and historical festivals. Many Hungarian holidays pay tribute to the struggles of their ancestors in securing the independence and freedom that Hungarians enjoy today.

January: January 1 is a public holiday. The **New Year** festivities traditionally include champagne and fireworks. In Budapest, the Roma community holds a large concert featuring a one hundred-person band. People relax after attending parties into the early morning hours the night before, enjoy the day off from work, and savor the last day of the holiday season.

March/April: March 15 commemorates the 1848 revolution against Austrian rule. This is a national holiday, and all banks and government offices are closed. **Easter Week** may fall in March or April, and the festival is celebrated throughout the country. **Easter** is celebrated on Sunday and again on **Easter Monday**, as the Monday following Easter is also a recognized national holiday.

May: Labor Day is celebrated on May 1. This holiday was once a communist holiday when workers were expected to celebrate the joys of work. Today in Hungary, it is a welcome day of rest and relaxation. **Whit Monday**, a religious festival, is celebrated fifty days after Easter and often falls in May.

July: July 1 marks **Civil Servants Day**, another holdover from the communist era. This day is set aside to recognize the hard work and important contributions of the nation's civil servants. In the days of communist rule, parades and demonstrations celebrated these workers, but today it is much like Labor Day, a day of leisure.

August: August 20 is the day that two important national holidays are celebrated, **St. Stephen's Day** celebrates the founding of the state and honors Saint Stephen, the first Christian king of Hungary, who ruled between 997 and 1038. It is also the **Festival of the New Bread**, and the first bread from the new harvest is baked especially for this day.

October: October 23 marks the **Day of the Proclamation of the Republic**. This holiday also pays tribute to the October 23, 1956, Hungarian uprising against Soviet occupation. In honor of the uprising, Hungary declared itself an independent republic on October 23, 1989.

November: All Saints' Day on November 1 is an important religious holiday in certain parts of the country. People remember and honor the dead on this day. Families gather together and decorate the graves of loved ones.

December: Christmas Day, December 25, is family time in Hungary and celebrated with large family gatherings, music, and food. **Boxing Day**, December 26, is also known as the second day of Christmas. This is a national holiday and is traditionally a day when gifts are exchanged between family and friends.

Goulash

This is perhaps the most famous Hungarian dish. Contrary to many recipes now popular in the West, authentic goulash is not made with tomato sauce.

Makes 6 servings

Ingredients
2 pounds beef chuck
1 teaspoon salt
2 onions, white or yellow
2 tablespoons lard or shortening
2 tablespoons sweet paprika
2 bay leaves
1 quart water
4 peeled and diced potatoes
1/4 teaspoon black pepper

Egg Dumplings
1 egg
6 tablespoons flour
1/8 teaspoon salt

Directions
Cut beef into 1-inch squares, add 1/2 teaspoon salt. Chop onions and brown in shortening, add beef and paprika. Let beef simmer in its own juice along with salt and paprika for 1 hour on low heat. Add water, diced potatoes, and remaining salt. Cover and simmer until potatoes are done and meat is tender. Prepare egg dumpling batter.

Add flour to unbeaten egg and salt. Mix well. Let stand for 1/2 hour to allow the flour gluten to relax. Drop by teaspoonful into goulash. Cover and simmer 5 minutes after dumplings rise to surface.

Serve hot with dollops of sour cream.

Hungarian Pancakes (Palacsinta)

Ingredients
4 whole well-beaten eggs
2 cups milk
2 teaspoons sugar
2 cups sifted flour
butter

Directions
Mix flour, salt and sugar. Combine well-beaten eggs and milk. Add egg and milk gradually to flour mixture, beating to a thin smooth batter. Let batter sit for a half hour. Place three spoonfuls of batter on a hot buttered skillet. Batter will be very thin. Tilt skillet quickly in a circular motion to distribute batter over skillet. Brown pancakes lightly on both sides. As each pancake is done, spread with strawberry jam, roll up lightly, and sprinkle with powdered sugar. Pancakes can be made ahead of time and reheated in a warm oven for a few minutes.

Hot Bacon Potato Salad (Sultszalonnas krumplisalata)

Ingredients
8 whole red potatoes washed
1 small onion
1/4 pound bacon
3 tablespoons vinegar
2 tablespoons flour
2 teaspoons sugar
1 teaspoons salt
1 cup water

Directions
Cook potatoes in boiling water until tender. Peel, and cut into slices. Place potatoes in mixing bowl. Dice bacon and fry until almost crisp. Remove diced bacon and place into mixing bowl with other ingredients. Peel and chop onion and place into reserved bacon fat. Sauté for a few minutes. Remove onion with slotted spoon and place into mixing bowl. Cook 2 tablespoons flour in fat from bacon until smooth and bubbly; then add 3 tablespoons vinegar, 2 teaspoons sugar, 1 teaspoon salt, and enough water to make about one cup of sauce. Bring to a boil and cook until sauce is thickened. Pour over ingredients in mixing bowl, and toss and mix.

PROJECT AND REPORT IDEAS

Maps

- Make a map of the eurozone, and create a legend to indicate key manufacturing industries throughout the EU.
- Create a map of Hungary using a legend to represent all the major tourist destinations within Hungary. The map should clearly indicate at least ten major tourist destinations.

Reports

- Write a brief report on Hungary's automobile industry.
- Hungarian Jews suffered greatly during World War II, in part because of Hungary's alliance with Nazi Germany. Write a brief report on the effects of World War II on Hungary's Jewish minority.
- Write a report on Hungary's role within the EU.
- Write a brief report on any of the following historical events: World War I, World War II, or the fall of communism in Hungary.

Journal

- Imagine you are a student in Hungary as the country begins the transition to democracy in 1988. Write a journal entry discussing your feelings about the great changes taking place in your country.
- Read more about composer Franz Liszt. Write a journal about your life and how life in Hungary inspires your music.

Projects

- Learn the Hungarian expressions for simple words such as hello, good day, please, and thank you. Try them on your friends.
- Make a calendar of your country's festivals and list the ones that are common or similar in Hungary. Are they celebrated differently in Hungary? If so, how?

- Go online or to the library and find images of an important Hungarian building. Create a model of it.
- Make a poster advertising a tourist destination in Hungary.
- Make a list of all the rivers, places, seas, and islands that you have read about in this book and indicate them on a map of Hungary.
- Find a Hungarian recipe other than the ones given in this book, and ask an adult to help you make it. Share it with members of your class.

Group Activities

- Debate: One side should take the role of Germany and the other Hungary. Germany's position is that the EU should adopt a supranational approach, while Hungary will speak in favor of the intergovernmental mode.
- Reenact the Hungarian Uprising of 1956.

CHRONOLOGY

1300 BCE	Invading Asian tribes wipe out the existing Bronze Age culture of the region.
400 CE	Romans are driven out by the Goths, who were conquered by the Huns.
900 CE	Magyars invade modern Hungary.
1001	Stephen I establishes the kingdom of Hungary as a Christian state.
1541	Hungary is divided between Austria and the Ottomans.
1718	All of Hungary is united under Hapsburg rule.
1848	The Revolution of 1848 begins as Hungarian nationalists revolt against the monarchy.
1849	Russia invades on behalf of Austria, and the Hapsburgs regain control.
1867	The Austro-Hungarian Empire is established.
1914	World War I begins.
1918	Germany is defeated in World War I.
1919	The Hungarian Socialist Republic is created.
1920	A secret election restores the monarchy, and Horthy is appointed regent.
1939	Germany invades Poland, and World War II begins.
1945	Allies defeat Germany in World War II.
1948–1949	Communist control of Hungary is solidified.
1956	The Hungarian Uprising against Soviet control is crushed.
1988	The Hungarian Parliament passes a "Democracy Package" of political reforms.
1989	Hungary declares itself an independent republic and establishes democracy.
1999	Hungary joins NATO.
2004	Hungary joins the EU.

Further Reading/Internet Resources

Hill, Raymond. *Hungary*. New York: Facts on File, Inc., 1997.

Lendvai, Paul, and Ann Major. *The Hungarians: A Thousand Years of Victory in Defeat*. Princeton, N.J.: Princeton University Press, 2004.

Molnar, Miklos, and Anna Magyar. *Concise History of Hungary*. New York: Cambridge University Press, 2001.

Popescu, Julian. *Hungary*. Philadelphia, Pa.: Chelsea House Publishers, 1999.

Ungvary, Krizstian, and Ladislaus Lob. *Siege of Budapest: One Hundred Days in World War II*. New Haven, Conn.: Yale University Press, 2005.

Travel Information
www.lonelyplanet.com/destinations/europe/hungary/
www.port.hu/kultura/index_a.html

History and Geography
www.infoplease.com
www.panda.org/dowloads/europe/huprofile.pdf

Culture and Festivals
www.budapesthotels.com
www.hungary.com
www.hunmagyar.org

Economic and Political Information
www.cia.gov/cia/publications/factbook/index.html
www.wikipedia.org

EU Information
europa.eu.int/

FOR MORE INFORMATION

Embassy of Hungary
3910 Shoemaker St., NW
Washington, DC 20008
Tel.: 202-362-6730

Embassy of the United States in Budapest
Szabadsag ter 12
H-1054 Budapest
Hungary
Tel.: 36-1-475-4400
Fax: 36-1-475-4764

European Union
Delegation of the European Commission to the United States
2300 M Street, NW
Washington, DC 20037
Tel.: 202-862-9500
Fax: 202-429-1766

Hungarian Ministry of Foreign Affairs
1027 Budapest
Bem rkp. 47.
Phone: 36-1-458-1000

Publisher's note:
The Web sites listed on this page were active at the time of publication. The publisher is not responsible for Web sites that have changed their addresses or discontinued operation since the date of publication. The publisher will review and update the Web-site list upon each reprint.

GLOSSARY

absolute rule: Rule completely free from constitutional or other restraint.

abstract: Not aiming to depict an object but composed with the focus on internal structure and form.

Age of Enlightenment: Period in the eighteenth century during which reason began to play an important role.

assimilated: Integrated somebody into a larger group so that differences were minimized.

autonomous: Able to act independently.

autonomy: Political independence and self-governance.

bloc: A group of united countries.

Bronze Age: A period of cultural history from between 3500 and 1500 BCE that was characterized by the use of tools made of bronze.

capital: Wealth in the form of money or property.

Celts: Members of an ancient Indo-European group who in pre-Roman times lived in central and western Europe.

centralization: Concentration of political or administrative power in a central power.

civil war: A war between opposing groups within a country.

communist: Supporter of communism, a classless society in which capitalism is overthrown by a working-class revolution that gives ownership and control of wealth and property to the state.

conifers: Trees with needle-shaped leaves that produce cones.

deciduous: Used to describe trees and shrubs that lose their leaves in the fall.

elite: A small group of people within a larger group who have more power, social standing, wealth, or talent than the rest of the group.

excise: A tax on goods used domestically.

feudal: Relating to the medieval European legal and social system in which vassals held land from lords in exchange for military service.

Goths: Members of an ancient Germanic people who settled in the south of the Baltic and between the third and fifth centuries founded kingdoms throughout the Roman Empire.

Great Depression: A severe decline in the world economy resulting in mass unemployment and widespread poverty that lasted from 1929 to approximately 1939.

gross domestic product (GDP): The total value of all goods and services produced within a country in a year.

infrastructure: Large-scale public systems, services, and facilities, such as roadways and utilities.

market economy: An economy in which prices and wages are determined mainly by the market and the laws of supply and demand.

migratory: Moving from one region to another every year, usually at specific times.

nationalism: Proud loyalty and devotion to a nation.

neutral: Not taking sides in a conflict.

nomadic: Characteristic of a group of people who wander from place to place.

op art: Optical art; mathematically based form of abstract art based on the repetition of simple shapes.

pagan: Someone who does not follow one of the world's main religions, especially somebody who is not Christian, Muslim, or Jewish, and whose religion is regarded as questionable.

passive: Tending not to participate actively.

privatization: The practice of transferring to private ownership an economic enterprise or public utility that had been under state ownership.

radical: representing extreme change from existing conditions.

ratified: Officially approved.

recession: A period of slow economic activity, not as severe as a depression.

regimented: Characterized by strict or excessive discipline.

reneged: Went back on a promise or commitment.

solidarity: The act of standing together, presenting a united front.

sovereignty: A politically independent state.

stagnancy: A state of inactivity in which no movement or development occurs.

surrealist: Someone who follows surrealism, an early twentieth-century movement that tried to represent the subconscious by creating fantastic imagery and juxtaposing elements that seem to contradict each other.

tariff: Tax levied by governments on goods, usually imports.

thermal lake: A lake with naturally heated water.

war reparations: Compensation demanded of a defeated nation by the winner of a war.

INDEX

PICTURE CREDITS

BIOGRAPHIES

AUTHOR

Heather Docalavich first developed an interest in the history and cultures of Eastern Europe through her work as a genealogy researcher. She currently resides in Hilton Head, South Carolina, with her four children.

SERIES CONSULTANT

Ambassador John Bruton served as Irish Prime Minister from 1994 until 1997. As prime minister, he helped turn Ireland's economy into one of the fastest-growing in the world. He was also involved in the Northern Ireland Peace Process, which led to the 1998 Good Friday Agreement. During his tenure as Ireland's prime minister, he also presided over the European Union presidency in 1996 and helped finalize the Stability and Growth Pact, which governs management of the euro. Before being named the European Commission Head of Delegation in the United States, he was a member of the convention that drafted the European Constitution, signed October 29, 2004.

The European Commission Delegation to the United States represents the interests of the European Union as a whole, much as ambassadors represent their countries' interests to the U.S. government. Matters coming under European Commission authority are negotiated between the commission and the U.S. administration.